DISNEY
PRINCESS

DELUXE PRINCESS
Music Player
STORYBOOK®

Belle's
Brave Friends

Reader's Digest Children's Books®

New York, New York • Montréal, Québec • Bath, UK

Belle's Brave Friends

Belle was outside enjoying the crisp, cool air, when she came upon a shivering, dirty puppy. She put out her hand and the puppy came toward her. Belle knew she had to get the puppy inside out of the cold, so she scooped him up and brought him into the castle.

Inside the castle, all of the enchanted objects laughed as the puppy splashed in the tub. Ottoman, the Beast's dog, tried to avoid getting wet!

8

When the puppy was clean and dry, Belle wanted to take him for a walk. The puppy reminded Ottoman what it was like to be a young dog. He wanted to go for a walk, too!

Outside, Ottoman ran into the woods. The puppy followed. Belle called for the dogs, but got no response. *Where could they be?* she thought, as she headed into the woods. It was getting dark, and the wind blew through the trees.

 Suddenly, Belle saw a strange shape and a pair of glowing eyes! She hurried away as quickly as she could.

13

As Belle walked into the woods, it got darker and darker. And she soon discovered that the eyes she had seen were those of a wolf—who belonged to a large pack of wolves! Thinking quickly, she used Lumiere to set fire to a large branch. Ottoman and the puppy crept up softly behind Belle.

The flaming branch scared away the wolves, but how long could she keep them at bay?

Suddenly, Belle tripped and the torch rolled out of reach. As the wolves came closer, Ottoman and the puppy sprang into action! The puppy picked up thc burning stick and chased the wolves away. He had saved Belle! The friends hurried out of the woods, glad to be reunited— and frce of the wolves!

As they left the woods, Belle and the dogs came upon the Beast, who had come out to find them. He was surprised to meet the new puppy, but when he heard how the brave dog had saved Belle, he knew the puppy belonged in the castle.

 Back inside, they all settled down by the cozy fire. The Beast petted Ottoman and the puppy, and fed them biscuits. Belle was glad that the Beast had welcomed the puppy into their home.

And the next night, as Belle and the Beast danced in the ballroom, the puppy and Ottoman proudly wore badges that proclaimed, "Protector of the House."